Teddy's Christmas Surprise

by Diane Stortz

Illustrated by Tim Bowers

Every year on December 1, Mother Bear said, "Time to get ready for Christmas!" So Mother Bear and Father Bear and Teddy Bear and Teddy's twin sisters swept and scrubbed and polished,

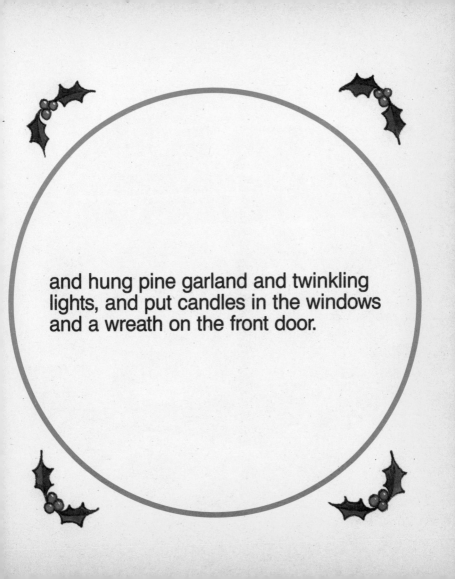

and hung pine garland and twinkling lights, and put candles in the windows and a wreath on the front door.

They decorated the Christmas tree and made cookies and candy to give to all their neighbors.

Then they planned the presents they would give to one another. Father made his presents in his workshop. Mother made her presents in her sewing room. And the twins went shopping at the mall. "I want to give presents too," said Teddy. "I'm big enough." "All right," said Mother. "Will you need any help?" "No," said Teddy. "I want my presents to be a Christmas surprise."

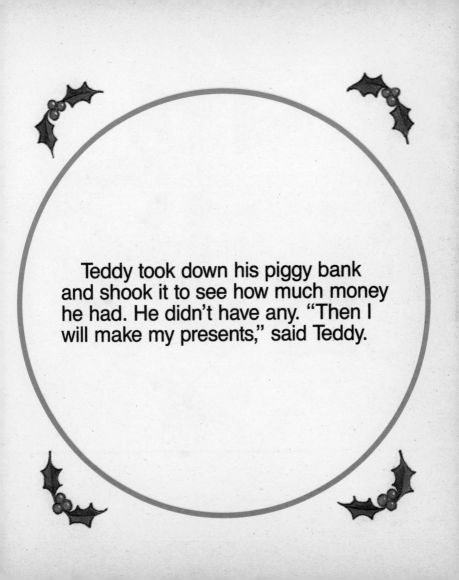

Teddy took down his piggy bank and shook it to see how much money he had. He didn't have any. "Then I will make my presents," said Teddy.

Teddy looked in Mother's craft closet. He looked in Mother's craft books. He tried very hard to follow the directions.

But Teddy's presents didn't turn out very well. "Now what will I do?" said Teddy. "What will I give for my Christmas surprise?"

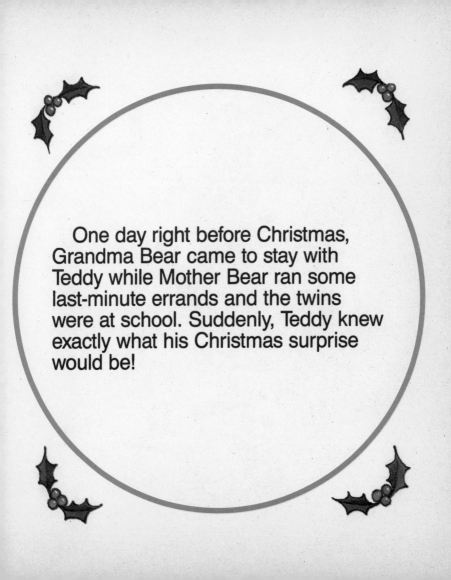

One day right before Christmas, Grandma Bear came to stay with Teddy while Mother Bear ran some last-minute errands and the twins were at school. Suddenly, Teddy knew exactly what his Christmas surprise would be!

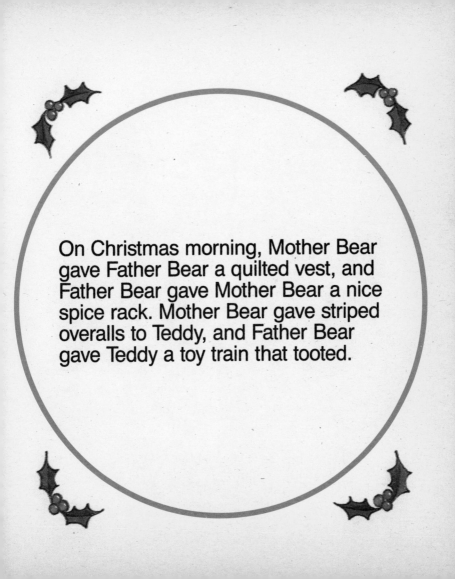

On Christmas morning, Mother Bear gave Father Bear a quilted vest, and Father Bear gave Mother Bear a nice spice rack. Mother Bear gave striped overalls to Teddy, and Father Bear gave Teddy a toy train that tooted.

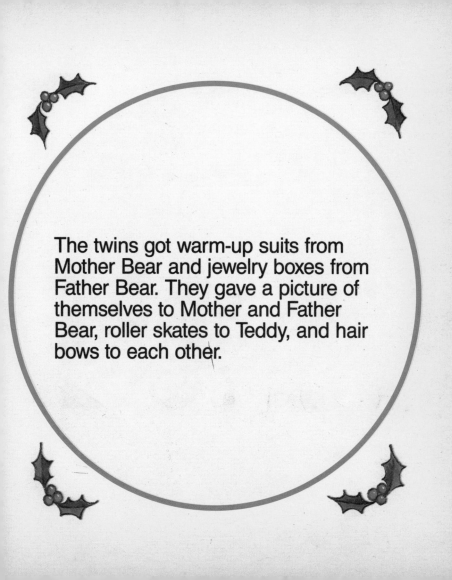

The twins got warm-up suits from Mother Bear and jewelry boxes from Father Bear. They gave a picture of themselves to Mother and Father Bear, roller skates to Teddy, and hair bows to each other.

"Where is your Christmas surprise, Teddy?" asked Mother Bear. "Come close and I will show you," said Teddy.

He gave everyone in his family a big Christmas bear hug!